It's five years since Ben Tennyson last transformed into aliens and fought crime with his cousin Gwen and their Grandpa Max.

Now 15 years old, Ben is once again forced to turn to the Omnitrix to help fight a new and more sinister threat – the HighBreed, DNAliens and the Forever Knights, who team up to take over the world.

The watch-like Omnitrix has re-programmed itself and has a complete set of ten, brand new alien choices for Ben to get to grips with. Helped by his cousin Gwen with her magical powers and Ben's former enemy, Kevin E. Levin, Ben is soon all set to go hero once again!

NOW READ ON . . .

EGMONT

We bring stories to life

This edition first published in Great Britain 2010
by Egmont UK Limited
239 Kensington High Street
London W8 6SA

Adapted by Barry Hutchison

1 3 5 7 9 10 8 6 4 2

Printed and bound in Great Britain

The Forest Stewardship Council (FSC) is an international,
non-governmental organisation dedicated to promoting
responsible management of the world's forests. FSC operates
a system of forest certification and product labelling that
allows consumers to identify wood and wood-based products
from well-managed forests.

For more information about Egmont's paper buying policy,
please visit www.egmont.co.uk/ethicalpublishing
For more information about the FSC, please visit their
website at www.fsc.org

BEN 10
ALIEN FORCE™

PIER PRESSURE

CHAPTER ONE

THE INVITATION

Fingers of smoke curled up from a deep trench that ran like a scar across the ground. It cut through fences and trees, churned up concrete and soil, before finally coming to an end in the middle of a field.

In the hole at the heart of the field, a damaged spaceship lay still. It was silent, aside from the faint pings made by the metal exterior as it slowly cooled down.

Underneath the ship, a black, oily liquid dripped down onto the ground. For a moment it looked as if the spacecraft had sprung a leak, but then the gloopy liquid squirmed out from beneath the ship, and up the side of the trench.

As the thing crawled along, a pattern of green circles formed on its black surface. The design looked strange and yet to anyone who had ever encountered the alien hero known as Upgrade, it would have looked very familiar.

Wriggling through the grass, the blob came to a busy motorway. Directly across from the field, a truck driver had just finished fixing a flat tyre. He stood back and wiped sweat from his brow.

He was so busy admiring his handiwork that he didn't notice the alien blob sneak up and squeeze through the radiator grille of the truck.

Once inside, the blob began to expand. It oozed across every piece of metal it touched, giving the engine the same black and green pattern as it had.

In just a few seconds the entire lorry was covered with the same design. The driver jumped back in fright when the truck roared noisily into life and sped off along the motorway.

'Hey!' bellowed the driver, giving chase. 'Where you going with my –?'

SCREEECH!

The lorry's brakes locked on, sending the entire vehicle into a sharp spin. When it was facing towards the driver again it lurched forwards, smoke pouring from the exhaust.

The driver stumbled backwards, shielding his face with his hands even though he knew it would do him no good. Through his fingers he spied something unbelievable. As the truck sped towards him it started changing. The entire engine bay split in two, opening up like a giant mouth.

The last thing the driver saw before closing his eyes was the mechanical mouth opening wider, revealing row after row of deadly green-and-black teeth!

Ben and Gwen were sat in the middle of a crowd of people, their heads turning left then right then left then right. An inter-school tennis match was taking place. A girl from Ben's school – Julie Yamamoto – was playing a girl from another school. It was a close game, but Julie had just edged into the lead.

As Julie got ready to serve, she spotted Ben. A smile spread across her face. She gave him a wave, before turning back to the game.

An even bigger smile broke out across Ben's face. Gwen couldn't help but notice. 'She waved. She likes you. You should ask her out.'

Ben blushed and looked down. 'No way. What if she finds out about the Omnitrix? I don't want her to think I'm weird.'

'Ben, you are weird,' Gwen pointed out. 'But you're also funny and sensitive and well-mannered. Unlike some people I know.'

Gwen turned around and looked behind her. Kevin was sprawled out across two chairs. His head was back and he was snoring loudly.

Suddenly, the crowd erupted in cheers as Julie hammered a shot past her opponent. Ben and Gwen leapt up, punching the air in delight. From behind them they heard Kevin splutter.

'What'd I miss?'

'She won!' said Ben, happily.

'Go ahead, Ben!' said Gwen, giving her cousin a friendly nudge. 'Now's your chance!'

'Uh, I'm not sure . . . aaghh!' Ben's sentence was cut short by Gwen pulling him down the steps towards the court.

Julie had just finished shaking hands with her opponent when Gwen shoved Ben towards her.

'Whoa!' Ben yelped, stumbling and almost falling at Julie's feet.

'Ben!' beamed Julie, pleased to see him.

'Julie, hey!' Ben replied, nervously.

'Good game, Julie!' said Gwen. She gave her cousin a pointed look. 'Ben?'

'Right, way to go,' Ben stammered. 'Great game. Match. Set. Whatever.' He swallowed hard, knowing what he wanted to say, but too afraid to say it. 'Well, see ya.'

Flashing another nervous smile, he turned on the spot, only for Gwen to catch him by the elbow and spin him back round.

'Back so soon?' asked Julie, grinning.

'Heh, so, um, Julie? I was wondering if you'd like to, I dunno, get together. Sometime.'

'Sure. When?'

Ben spun around to face his cousin, his eyes wide with panic. 'She said "when?". That's like a yes, only more specific,' he whispered. 'Now what?'

'You say, "how about tonight?".'

Ben's face went pale. 'Tonight?' he said, in a voice that was barely more than a squeak. Gwen nodded, and so Ben turned back to Julie, trying to act as naturally as possible. 'Ahem, I mean, we could go to the pier. Tonight.'

Julie nodded. 'Great!'

Ben stood there, nodding and smiling, not entirely sure what he should say next.

'Well,' began Julie at last. 'Guess I'll hit the showers.'

'Yes!' cried Ben, relieved not to have to think of something to say. 'Good. Me too. I mean, er . . . '

'He'll come by around seven,' said Gwen, stepping in to save her cousin from embarrassing himself even more. 'Sometimes I wonder,' she muttered, as she dragged him towards the exit, 'how the species survives.'

A few miles away, a policeman stood by the side of the road, looking down at the wreckage of an eighteen-wheeler truck. He spoke into his radio.

'Yeah, I found that stolen truck. No, no sign of whoever took it.'

Behind the officer, a squidgy black and green blob squirmed over to his police car and climbed inside it. In moments, the alien pattern had swept over the entire vehicle.

'Whaddya mean, "he says it drove away by himself"?' snorted the policeman in reply to someone on the other end of the radio. 'That just doesn't happen.'

VROOOM! The police car's engine roared loudly.

' . . . much,' added the policeman, flatly, as he watched his car speed off into the distance.

Ben stared at his reflection in his bedroom mirror. He was not pleased with what he saw.

'Great. My hair looks stupid, my shirt is wrinkled, and I have a zit the size of Kansas.'

'Yeah, that's one big zit alright.'

Ben wheeled around to find Kevin standing behind him, grinning.

'How did you get in here?'

'The usual way,' replied Kevin, holding up a fist. It shone like polished metal. 'You may want to fix that hole I punched in your back door before your mother sees it.'

Ben sighed. 'You couldn't knock?'

'I sort of did.'

'Has anyone ever told you that you're a strange and dangerous person?' asked Ben.

'Constantly. But enough about me. Gwen says you need a favour.'

'Uh, yeah. See, I kinda want to go to the pier tonight with Julie.'

'I bet you do,' smirked Kevin.

'And since I don't have a car –'

'Or a licence,' Kevin reminded him.

'Or a licence,' Ben nodded. He hesitated. Why was he even bothering to ask? There was no way Kevin would agree to it. 'Well, so I was wondering if you could, um, maybe give us a ride to the pier?'

For a moment Kevin said nothing. Finally, he shrugged his shoulders. 'OK.'

Ben's eyes went wide with surprise. 'That's it? No jokes, no insults, no blackmail?'

'Nope.'

'Wow. Thanks,' began Ben, before a thought occurred to him. 'Wait. You're gonna wait till we're in the car and then you're going to make my life miserable, aren't you?'

A wicked smile spread across Kevin's

face, but he didn't say anything as he turned and walked out of the bedroom.

'This should be fun,' Ben muttered, before setting off after Kevin, ready for his date with Julie.

CHAPTER TWO

CAR TROUBLE

Kevin's car cut through the early-evening traffic on the way to the pier. Gwen sat in the front passenger seat, with Ben and Julie sitting in the back.

'Now remember, little Benny boy,' said Kevin, in the voice of a controlling dad he'd once seen in a television show, 'your mother and I want you home by ten o'clock sharp, or you can't go to the disco!'

Julie blinked, confused. 'Disco?'

Ben shook his head, indicating she should ignore Kevin. 'He watches a lot of repeats,' he explained.

'Give him a break, Kevin,' said Gwen.

'Gosh, pumpkin, what do you mean?' Kevin asked, still using the same goofy voice.

'You know exactly what I mean,' Gwen whispered. 'At least when Ben likes a girl he lets her know. He asks her out. Maturity, isn't that a novel approach?'

Kevin thought about this for a moment, before launching into song. 'Ben's got a girlfriend, Ben's got a girlfriend!'

Ben groaned loudly as Kevin continued to sing. Neither of them noticed the police car cruising along the street just thirty or so metres behind them – or the fact that it had nobody behind the wheel.

When Ben and Julie stepped out of Kevin's car, they had no idea they were being watched. Further along the street, the green-and-black police car was doing its best to hide behind a lamppost. Its headlights blinked like eyes as it watched Kevin's car drive away, and saw Ben and Julie stroll on to the pier.

The pier itself was a fairground-type attraction, with games, rides and stalls filling every available space. On some nights it was almost impossible to move for people. Tonight was not one of those nights.

'Listen, uh, sorry about Kevin,' muttered Ben, as he and Julie walked along.

'Why is he so mean to you?'

'It makes him happy.'

Julie giggled. 'You're nice to let him.'

Ben smiled and looked around properly

for the first time. 'Slow night. This place is packed on weekends.'

'Good,' said Julie, brightly. She slipped her arm through Ben's. 'This way we have the place to ourselves.'

'Yeah,' said Ben, smiling from ear to ear. 'Guess we do.'

BE-DEEP! BE-DEEP! BE-DEEP!

Ben stared down at the Omnitrix. It was emitting a high-pitched screeching sound he'd never heard it make before.

'Is that a watch?' Julie asked, stepping back and covering her ears.

'Heh, yeah,' Ben replied. 'Really have to get it fixed. You like candy floss?' he asked, then spoke again before she had a chance to reply. 'Good, you stay here, I'll be back!'

Without another word, he turned and ran off between two stalls, leaving Julie alone, and a little confused.

When he was safely out of sight, Ben gave the Omnitrix a shake, trying to make it shut up. 'Typical,' he muttered. 'Everything's going great then this freaks out on me.'

Over by the entrance to the pier, the green-and-black blob slithered on to the boardwalk. It's alien sensors locked on to Ben and the Omnitrix immediately, and for a moment it just sat there, watching the boy shake the watch violently up and down.

At last the blob turned and fixed its gaze on the bumper cars, where some people were having fun crashing into one another. Moving as quickly as its slug-like body would allow, the blob crawled towards the dodgems.

Ben, meanwhile, was trying another technique with the Omnitrix. He was slamming it against the wooden stall he was hiding behind. On the fifth smack, the alarm fell silent.

'That's more like it,' said Ben, quietly, before a panicked scream from the bumper car ride shattered his new-found silence.

Ben looked up to see a bumper car leaping over the barrier surrounding the ride. It thudded down on to the wooden pier, then barrelled towards him, its one headlight blazing like the eye of a Cyclops.

The sparkling lights of the fair reflected off the shiny green-and-black surface of the car as it reared up so it stood as tall as Ben himself. Then, to Ben's surprise and horror, a wide gap appeared in the car's surface, just below the headlight. The gap widened, revealing several large and lethal-looking teeth.

As the shadow of the bumper car passed over him, Ben swallowed hard, 'That seriously cannot be good.'

The car lurched closer and closer and Ben had to dodge sideways to avoid being splattered. Turning, he ran from the car, powering along the deserted pier as fast as his legs would carry him.

Over the thudding of his footsteps Ben heard another sound. An electric engine revved and whined behind him, getting louder as the dodgem drew nearer. He wanted to look back over his shoulder to see how close the car was, but to do that would mean slowing down, and slowing down seemed like a very bad idea.

Ben came to a corner where the rows of sideshows ran off in another direction. Catching the side of one of the stalls he swung himself around without slowing. He heard the squeal of brakes and felt the pier shudder as the bumper car skidded and crashed into the wall of a shop.

Still Ben ran. Bumper cars were built for crashing. There was no way a little collision like that would slow this one down.

Sure enough, just a few seconds later Ben heard the whine of the engine once again. Tucking his head down he pushed himself to go faster, ignoring the burning pain in his legs.

A candy floss stand seemed to loom up out of nowhere, right in Ben's path. Too close to go around it, Ben could only leap up on to the stand and hurl himself off the other side. The candy floss seller ducked as Ben came bounding over the top of him.

'Watch it!' he cried, angrily.

KA-RUNCH!

The bumper car clipped the corner of the cart, sending it into a spin. The candy floss seller yelped as he was knocked down on to his bottom on the hard wooden pier. He eyed his damaged cart as it slowly stopped spinning.

Someone would have to pay for this – and he knew just who to blame!

Thirty metres away, the car skidded around another corner and stopped. The part of the pattern that looked most like a face pulled into a frown as the vehicle's alien scanners searched for Ben. They panned left and right, sweeping over the entire area, but could find no trace of him anywhere.

Way up high, almost directly above the bumper car, Ben clung tightly to the side of a tall ride. He watched the car below, hardly daring to even breathe. 'What is this?' he whispered. 'When Carnival Rides Attack?'

At the back of the bumper car a long metal pole – usually used to connect to the electrical circuit that powers the dodgems – began to glow an eerie shade of blue. As Ben looked on, circles of green light rose from the tip of the pole. Ben almost lost his grip when he guessed what was happening. The dodgem car was sending out some kind of homing signal. And that meant –

BE-DEEP! BE-DEEP! BE-DEEP!

Once again the Omnitrix emitted a piercing alarm.

'Ssh!' Ben urged, releasing his grip for long enough to give the watch a sharp shake. But the alarm continued, and from up on the side of the ride Ben saw the bumper car twist to look in his direction.

VROOM!

The dodgem sprung forwards, its wheels spraying smoke. Ben braced himself, gripping on tightly as the car raced straight towards the ride he was clinging to.

The front of the bumper car struck the metal structure, sending vibrations all the way to the top. Despite all his efforts, Ben's fingers weren't strong enough to hold on. He toppled backwards, his arms reaching out, clawing at the air as he fought to find something to catch on to.

It was no use. Screaming, Ben fell away from the carnival ride and plummeted backwards towards the ground below.

CHAPTER THREE

EL MATADOR

WHUUMP!

Ben landed hard in the passenger seat of the bumper car. He wasn't sure if this was good news or bad news. It was good that he hadn't splattered on to the ground, but now he was at the mercy of the possessed car, which had begun to race along the pier the second he had landed. Still, at least the Omnitrix had stopped screaming at him. For now.

The speed of the car made the wind sting Ben's eyes as he stood up in the seat. 'OK,' he said, fixing his gaze on a rope that was strung across the boardwalk up ahead, 'I am so over this!'

Hurling himself into the air, Ben caught hold of the rope and swung upwards. The bumper car accelerated beneath him, leaving him behind. Ben dropped silently down on to the wooden pier and whipped off his jacket. If the car wanted a fight, he'd give it one!

'Hey, bumpo, bumpo!' he cried, twirling his jacket around like a bull-fighter's cape. The bumper car skidded around so it was facing him and immediately began to charge.

The whine of the electric motor grew louder and louder in Ben's ears. The car was already almost upon him, but he couldn't move yet. He had to hold his nerve for just a few seconds more . . .

Now!

Ben whipped the jacket away at the last possible second, revealing a solid metal post bolted to a concrete block that was set into the floor of the pier. The car had no time to stop, no chance of avoiding the head-on crash.

The car folded around the metal pole as if its bonnet were made of modelling clay. While the front half of the dodgem stopped instantly, the back end kept on going, collapsing the entire vehicle in on itself.

As Ben watched, the green-and-black pattern that had been covering the car faded away, returning the vehicle to its original colour, if not its original shape.

'I hope there's a simple explanation for this,' Ben said. 'But I doubt it.'

A sharp squeaking sound from his left made Ben turn. The candy floss seller limped along the pier, dragging his badly damaged cart behind him. The man did not look in the slightest bit happy.

'Kid, you and me got a date with my insurance adjuster,' he growled.

A jolt of panic shot through Ben. 'Date!' he cried. 'Aaaah!'

Reaching into the cart, Ben grabbed two sticks of candy floss. 'Look, here's my allowance,' he said, handing the salesman a ten dollar bill. 'It's all I've got.'

'And then he ran off,' said Julie, speaking into her mobile phone, 'and I've been . . . wait, he's coming back. Later.'

Ben clattered to a halt beside her, out of breath from running so far.

'Sorry,' he panted. 'You would not believe that queue.'

Julie glanced around. 'Ben, there's nobody here.'

'Um, except at the concession stand, where they've been doing huge business,' replied Ben, smiling a little too broadly.

'I thought you'd stood me up,' said Julie, glancing down at her feet.

Ben looked shocked. 'Julie,' he said, 'I'd never, ever do that to you.'

He held out the candy floss and smiled again – for real this time. 'Look, I got pink and blue. Your pick.'

took the pink stick. She picked some off and popped it in her mouth, while Ben opened his jaws and chomped down on a huge piece of his own candy floss. She giggled when he opened his mouth again, revealing two rows of bright blue teeth.

Ben gave a faint sigh of relief. Maybe this date wouldn't be a complete disaster after all.

A few miles away, in a deep crater in a dark field, a solitary figure shuffled around the fallen spaceship.

PiNG. PiNG. PiNG. PiNG.

A warning light blinked on a control panel, slow at first, but gradually becoming faster and louder. The figure hobbled closer and reached a hand out to touch the panel.

'Aaaaaargh!' he howled in pain as ribbons

of electric-blue energy wrapped around his hand and danced up his arm.

Anyone crossing the field would have heard the cries and seen the flickering blue glow of the electricity. But there was no one crossing the field. No one to see the light or hear the cries.

The figure in the ship was alone. Alone and screaming in the darkness.

Julie and Ben stood at the foot of some metal stairs, looking up at a full-sized replica of an F-15 fighter jet. The jet was fixed in place by a large metal pole. It moved up and down, left and right, making the fighter plane buck and thrash around.

'This looks fun,' said Julie.

'Especially if you don't mind wrenching

G-forces and waves of nausea,' said Ben,
nodding enthusiastically.

Julie laughed. 'Are you saying you don't
want to ride it?'

'No, I'm saying it's a good thing I didn't
get us cheeseburgers!' said Ben, before a
movement on the surface of the aeroplane
caught his attention. The shiny silver surface
of one wing was taking on the black-and-green
appearance. It was the same pattern he'd seen
on the bumper car, and that could only mean
one thing . . . trouble.

'Uh-oh.'

'You OK?' asked Julie.

'Me? Fine. No problem,' said Ben, quickly.
'Listen, maybe we should skip this one?'

'Ben Tennyson, are you hiding
something?' Julie teased.

'No, no secrets here,' Ben babbled, 'my
life's an open book, just your basic regular guy.'

The alien pattern finished covering the

jet fighter, and the entire ride rippled like the surface of a lake. With a sudden burst of flame from its engines, the giant model aeroplane rose up and tilted so its nose was pointed directly at the couple.

'Here we go again,' Ben groaned.

The jet made a lunge for Ben, clamping its wings shut almost as if it were clapping a pair of enormous hands. The metal slammed together just centimetres from Ben's head, making Julie scream with fright. Ben caught her by the arm and dragged her away from the ride, shouting, 'This way!'

They hurried along the boardwalk, Ben in front, Julie being pulled along behind him. Ducking behind a wooden hut, Ben yanked open the door and pushed Julie inside.

'You stay here for a minute.'

'Where are you going?'

Ben hesitated. 'Uh, bathroom?'

Julie was about to say something but Ben didn't give her the chance. Slamming the door closed he pulled up his sleeve and turned the dial on the Omnitrix.

'This looks like a job for Jet Ray!'

CHAPTER FOUR

ALL THE FUN OF THE FAIR

A split-second before Ben could activate the Omnitrix, the jet fighter tore free from its support and screamed over his head. As Ben fell to the floor, he slammed his hand down on the watch.

The transformation began. Six legs sprouted out of his body. Two giant crab pincers appeared where his arms had been.

'Hey, this isn't Jet Ray,' Ben said, then quickly realising that he was thinking more clearly than ever before. 'Brain Storm!'

THWACK!

The jet fighter swooped down low, catching the crab-alien with a glancing blow to the top of his shell. Brain Storm flipped over and rolled clumsily along the pier, his claws clattering against the wood.

'Now,' he seethed when he finally tumbled to a stop on the boardwalk, 'I am most decidedly miffed.'

The entire top section of the alien's shell unfolded, revealing a bulging pink brain. Sparks bristled on the brain's surface, before coming together to form a funnel of devastating energy.

The first shot tore past the jet fighter, scorching the air just to its left. A second blast found its target, burning a hole clean through one of the aeroplane's wings.

For a moment the plane looked like it

was going down, before jets of flame from its afterburners pulled it around in a loop-the-loop.

Brain Storm stopped firing and watched as the plane banked down towards him. A strange green glow lit up the tips of its wings. 'What the deuce?' the crab-alien wondered aloud, before bolts of green energy began raining down on him from above.

Shutting his eyes, Brain Storm managed to throw up a force field around himself. The jet fighter's energy bolts bounced off the shield, striking surrounding huts instead.

The door to one hut creaked open and Julie poked her head out. She could hardly believe what she saw. A giant crab was standing a few metres away, and a jet fighter was firing something directly towards her!

A shimmering force field suddenly encased Julie, protecting her from the blasts of green energy which tore through the hut.

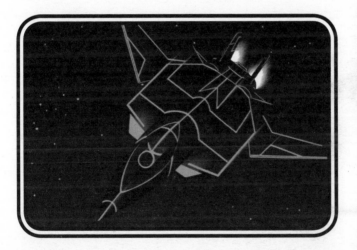

As Brain Storm's force field carried Julie to safety, the jet fighter's scanners locked on to her, analysing her from head to toe. When its scan was complete the plane rolled in mid-air and banked sharply towards the farthest end of the pier, where Julie was now standing unprotected.

KZAAAAP!

A coil of energy blasted from within Brain Storm's brain, almost splitting the jet in half. Its engines died instantly. Pouring smoke from its tail-end, the plane nose-dived down on to the pier.

In pieces it slid along the wooden planks, throwing up sparks as it hurtled towards the metal safety barrier. Before it hit the barrier, its wings clipped a towering swing ride, bringing the whole structure down on top of it.

Tangled together, the jet and the carnival ride smashed through the safety barrier and plunged down into the icy cold water below.

Brain Storm gave a satisfied nod. 'And good riddance, might I say?'

A few moments and a quick transformation later, Ben emerged from the men's bathroom and raced to find Julie.

'Did I miss anything?' he asked.

'You didn't see that?' spluttered Julie.

'See what?'

With a thunderous splash, the swing ride rose up from the water behind Ben, the alien pattern covering every part of it.

'Erm, that!' cried Julie, pointing upwards.

The structure loomed like a giant robot, the swinging seat pods attached to each of its four metal arms poised like huge fists, ready to smash down. Before Ben could fully understand what he was seeing, one of the fists swung down at him. Instinctively he ducked. Julie, however, wasn't so lucky.

'Ben!' she screamed, as the seating cage snapped shut around her, trapping her inside. She screamed for a second time when the ride lurched suddenly upwards, lifting her high above the pier.

Moving unsteadily, the living fairground ride stepped up on to the boardwalk. Ben felt the pier bend beneath him. He threw himself sideways, trying to make it to safety before –

SNAP!

The boards around him broke and he felt the world lurch sickeningly to one side. He threw his hands out, reaching for something – anything – that would help slow his fall.

His fingers found something solid. He looked up and discovered he was holding on to the edge of a broken plank. He didn't dare look down at the swirling waters beneath him.

Above the screams of the people on the pier, Ben heard Julie shouting his name. The carnival ride was stomping off through the water, towards the outskirts of the city.

Ben looked at the Omnitrix. He was holding on with his other hand, meaning he didn't have any fingers free to activate the watch. As the giant robot marched further away, and Julie's cries became fainter and fainter, Ben shook his head in despair.

'This,' he said, 'is just not my night.'

And with that, he let go, barely leaving himself enough time to gulp down a deep breath before he plunged beneath the surface of the water.

Unseen by anyone on the pier, a flash of green Omnitrix energy lit up the waves. A moment later Jet Ray leapt out of the water and soared upwards, like a mutant flying fish.

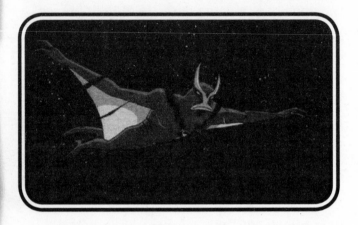

'None of this makes sense,' he muttered, 'Why am I being attacked by carnival rides? And why'd it grab Julie?'

Cars weaved out of the way, horns blaring, as the mutant swing ride thundered along the motorway.

Above it all, Jet Ray glided in, working on a plan as he surveyed the scene.

He spotted some lampposts up ahead. Firing his energy blasts, Jet Ray brought two of the metal poles toppling down across the road directly in front of the carnival ride. The lampposts caught on one of its mechanical feet, forcing it to stop.

The sudden halt sent its arms flailing wildly, forcing Julie to cling to the safety bar across her lap to avoid being thrown out. Jet Ray flew towards her, trying to reach her before the swing ride realised what was going on.

Too late!

Another of the pods tumbled through the sky and hit Jet Ray hard. He crashed down to Earth, buried beneath the twisted metal.

Jet Ray's claws made short work of the pod, and in just a few seconds he was back up. But there was one small problem. The carnival ride was gone.

And so was Julie.

CHAPTER FIVE

THE SHIPS

Jet Ray rocketed towards the sky, spinning around and around, searching for any sign of the mechanical monster and –

There! The swing ride was racing through a forest, heading in the direction of a field. From up high, Jet Ray could see the deep trench cut into the field, but that didn't matter right now. Only one thing mattered. Julie.

Soaring on his leathery wings, Jet Ray gave chase. By the time he caught up with the runaway ride, it was squatting in the middle of the field by the end of the trench. Julie, however, was nowhere to be seen.

'What have you done with Julie?' Jet Ray snarled.

'I'm here!' Julie stepped out from behind one of the swing-ride's legs, brushing dust from her clothes. 'And how do you know my name?'

Oops. How was he going to talk his way out of this one? There was only one thing for it. It was time for the truth, even if that did make her think he was a freak.

'Julie, don't be scared,' Jet Ray said, landing softly in front of her. 'It's me. It's Ben. I'm not going to hurt you.'

'You're a monster?' Julie gasped.

'No. Well, yes,' Jet Ray admitted. 'Actually, I'm like ten monsters.'

The alien hung his head, too ashamed to look at her.

'Cool!'

Jet Ray raised his eyes to see Julie smiling. In a flash he transformed back to Ben. 'Cool?' he repeated, stepping closer.

Before Julie could answer, the fairground ride loomed over them and began to emit high-pitched squeals. The sounds changed, before becoming something resembling a human voice.

'Ship ship ship ship ship!' it said.

'Excuse me, we're talking,' Ben said.

'I think it's trying to tell you something.'

The ride nudged Ben with the side of its foot. 'Ship ship ship,' it chirped.

Shifting its weight to the side, the ride pointed to the trench, where the alien craft lay.

'Ship. You've brought us out here to find that spaceship,' Ben realised. 'Right?'

He glanced up at the swing ride in time to see the black-and-green pattern fade away, revealing the original colours beneath. Slowly, the metal frame collapsed.

Ben clambered down into the trench and edged closer to the spacecraft. A large hole had been torn in one side, and through it he could see a familiar-looking alien figure trapped beneath some fallen machinery.

'I've seen that thing before,' he said.

'You have?' Julie frowned.

'Kinda. I . . . used to be able to turn into one of those. Called myself "Upgrade".'

The alien gave a whimper of pain.

'Well whatever it is, it's hurt,' said Julie, moving towards the ship. She stopped when Ben held his arm out. He nodded towards the faint red glow surrounding the spacecraft.

'You get any closer to that energy field and it'll fry you like a potato,' he warned.

Julie nodded and peered inside the ship. A monitor displayed a series of strange alien symbols. Each one flashed red on the screen.

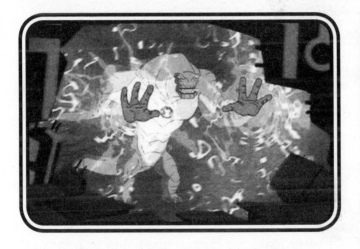

'What's that say?'

'Sorry, I don't read alien,' Ben confessed.

Down by his leg, Ben felt something bump against him. He looked down to find a black-and-green blob nudging him on the shin. 'So you're what's behind all this?' he said.

'Ship!' yelped the little alien goo-ball.

Ben shrugged. 'OK. "Ship".'

Ship wriggled backwards. With a ripple of its gloopy body, it moulded itself into the shape of the crashed spacecraft. Julie was about to applaud when the miniature version of the spaceship exploded in a shower of goo.

As Ship pulled himself back together, Julie turned to Ben. 'OK, now I know he's trying to tell you something!'

'It's a countdown,' Ben gasped, watching the symbols on the monitor count down. 'That thing's gonna explode!'

There was no time to waste. Slapping the Omnitrix, Ben transformed himself into the mighty Humungousaur and thundered towards the damaged vessel.

Pulling aside debris, Humungousaur found the cause of the problem. A damaged engine core hung from its housing. Its energy

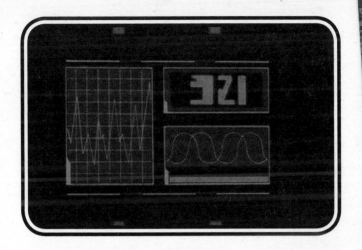

coils had been exposed, triggering a meltdown.

Moving quickly, the dino-alien ripped the engine core free and hurled it skyward.

BADOOOOOM!

The engine core went off like a bomb. Sparks shot like fireworks in all directions.

Humungousaur knelt down and wrapped his arms around Julie, cradling her protectively until long after the blast had died away.

'Um, explosion's over,' said Julie, smiling.

Humungousaur released her and stood up. 'Right,' he muttered. Even through his thick

orange skin, there was no way for the dino-alien
to hide the fact that he was blushing!

'There you go,' said Humungousaur,
lifting the fallen equipment from the alien pilot.

'Yes. Well, as I was saying,' began
the pilot, getting to his feet. 'I extruded this
symbiont, the one you call "Ship" –'

'Ship! Ship!' chattered the blob.

'I sent it off to find the nearest Plumber.'

Julie frowned. 'Because your sink was clogged?'

'Plumbers are intergalactic police officers,' Humungousaur told her. 'I'll explain later.' He turned back to the alien. 'And that's why it came after me?'

'Of course. Didn't you receive its signal?'

'You mean the beeping?'

'Yes, the "beeping",' the pilot grimaced. 'Don't you know how the Omnitrix works?'

'Not so much. No.'

'Really?' asked the pilot, surprised. 'Aren't you a Plumber?'

'No, I thought you were.'

'Spend the rest of my life here?' the alien muttered to himself, shuddering at the thought. 'Look, is there anyone else I can talk with?'

'Not really.'

'That's why Ship tried to get your attention.'

Green light flickered as Humungousaur changed back to Ben. 'Get my attention? He wrecked the pier! He kidnapped Julie!'

'Well, I needed help,' sniffed the pilot.

'That's pretty obvious,' Ben replied.

'And you wonder why most aliens only communicate with your livestock,' the pilot grumbled. 'Now, I must repair my warp drive.'

Julie flashed a friendly smile. 'Anything we can do to help?'

Hours later, Ben and Julie were doing their best to reattach an antenna to the ship.

'There, it's on tight,' said Julie, proudly.

Ben nodded, 'I, uh, I guess this is probably the worst date you've ever had, huh?'

'No. Just different,' Julie replied, resting a hand on his arm. 'And being different is fine.'

A hatch swung open between them. 'Right. All done,' announced the pilot. 'Off I go.'

Ben and Julie hopped down, almost landing on Ship, who was rolling in the dirt.

'What about this thing?' asked Ben. 'Doesn't he blorp back into your body?'

'That's not how it works. Besides, you and he have had such a lovely bonding experience. He's yours now.'

Ben and Julie watched the alien craft rise into the air and streak off towards the far reaches of outer space. They turned their attention down to the blob by Ben's side.

'He's cute,' Julie teased. 'Are you going to keep him?'

Ben didn't answer. There was too much going on in his head at that moment for him to find words. He knew they had a long walk to get back to town. He knew they would both be in big trouble with their parents, but despite all that – despite everything that had happened at the pier – Ben couldn't help but think that tonight had been the best night of his life!

'Come on,' he said, looking from Julie to Ship and back again. 'Let's go home.'